Trapped in Battle Royale
Book One

CLASH AT FATAL FIELDS

AN UNOFFICIAL NOVEL OF FORTNITE

Devin Hunter

Sky Pony Press
New York

Copyright © 2018 by Hollan Publishing, Inc.

All rights reserved. No part of this book may be reproduced in any manner
without the express written consent of the publisher, except in the case of
brief excerpts in critical reviews or articles. All inquiries should be addressed
to Sky Pony Press, 307 West 36th Street, 11th Floor, New York, NY 10018.

Sky Pony Press books may be purchased in bulk at special discounts for sales
promotion, corporate gifts, fund-raising, or educational purposes. Special
editions can also be created to specifications. For details, contact the Special
Sales Department, Sky Pony Press, 307 West 36th Street, 11th Floor,
New York, NY 10018 or info@skyhorsepublishing.com.

Sky Pony® is a registered trademark of Skyhorse Publishing, Inc.®,
a Delaware corporation.

Visit our website at www.skyponypress.com.

10 9 8 7 6 5 4 3 2

Library of Congress Cataloging-in-Publication Data is available on file.

Cover design by Brian Peterson
Cover artwork by Amanda Brack

Paperback ISBN: 978-1-5107-4263-5
E-book ISBN: 978-1-5107-4266-6

Printed in Canada

CHAPTER 1

Grey and his friends watched the clock as they waited out the last minutes of school. Usually it was Finn who was the most antsy, but today it was Grey. And not just because it was the last day of school.

"Log in to Discord so we can talk," Finn said. "It'll be easier to teach you that way."

"Okay," Grey said, as the seconds stretched out. "It's under my dad's name, but I'll find you."

"Cool. This will be awesome." Finn gave a wicked grin. "Though you'll probably be a total noob and get me killed."

"I'll be able to beat you soon! I have all summer to practice," Grey said. They both laughed, and the bell rang out their freedom. "See you online!"

"See ya!" Finn ran for the buses, but Grey lived close enough to school to walk. He raced back home after the last day of sixth grade. Today was the day he would finally get to play Fortnite like the rest of his friends. He had gotten the perfect grades that his parents demanded, and he hadn't fought with his younger sister even when she annoyed him on purpose. His father had downloaded the *Battle Royale* version last night, promising Grey could play the moment he got home from school.

Bursting through the front door, he raced to the computer in the living room. It was an old computer, and kind of laggy. But Grey didn't care. Grey turned it on and bounced with excitement as the screen lit up.

"Only for an hour, Grey!" his mother called from the kitchen.

"Okay!" He logged into Fortnite, ready to join the epic fights his friends were always talking about, but then an unexpected window popped up on the screen.

Updating Program . . .

Grey groaned. How could there already be an update when he just got it last night? This would eat into his time to play, and he didn't have much as it was. The update bar barely budged at first, thanks to his slow computer, but then it started to move faster near the end. He placed his hand on the mouse, ready to make a profile and drop onto the island for the very first time.

Finn would be waiting for him to get on Discord. Grey would do that after the update. Finn would teach him the ropes—he'd been playing since the game came out. Grey already knew a little bit, having watched Finn play when they hung out. Finn's favorite place to start was Fatal Fields. Finn would pretend to be a noob, but then he'd kill the few other players there and take the loot for himself. Grey thought his friend was clever, though maybe a little mean for hunting noobs. Even still, it would be nice to have Finn's help and protection.

Finally, the update finished and Grey clicked "Launch." As he did, his vision grew fuzzy. He tried to rub his eyes, but his hands felt numb and he couldn't tell if he was moving his arms at all.

"Ugh." He felt like he might throw up, and now was not the time to get sick. Grey tried to concentrate on the screen, but his head spun as well as his vision.

He looked down at his hands and gasped.

They looked like they were going invisible, but even worse, it seemed like they were getting sucked into his computer screen. It felt like his body was falling, and yet his face moved closer to the screen. Just when he felt like he'd lose his lunch, everything went black.

CHAPTER 2

Grey didn't know how much time had passed when he woke up, but he had probably wasted his whole hour of Fortnite play. When he opened his eyes, he expected to see his room. Maybe his mom would be there checking on him, since he was obviously sick. She had to have found him lying on the floor by the computer. Worst-case scenario, he worried he'd see a hospital room. He'd never passed out before, but he'd heard it could be serious.

He wasn't in his room *or* at the hospital.

His mother was nowhere to be found.

As he took in the large open space—something that looked like an old, rusty warehouse from a video game—he was surprised to find a crowd of people staring back at him. They were of all different ages and races, boys and girls, but one thing they all had in common: No one was smiling.

The people glared as if they were sizing him up, and as he pulled himself off the cement, his cheeks reddened under the scrutiny. He ran a hand through his brown hair, looking away from the crowd.

Did he look strange?

His hands looked the same size, and his skin was still a tan color. He was wearing the same t-shirt and shorts he had on when he sat down. He touched his face—there was nothing out of the ordinary.

That was when Grey realized he wasn't the only one facing them. There were four others standing by him who appeared equally confused. The girl on his right looked to be about his age, with black hair in a ponytail long enough to reach her waist. The guy on his left was older, at least in high school, and he towered over Grey in both height and width. Grey only wished that much more that he had hit his growth spurt.

"What's going on here?" The question came from the man standing on the other side of the girl. He looked to be as old as Grey's dad, with gray in his dark hair and beard.

In response, a woman appeared out of thin air right in front of them. Grey jumped back in surprise. He couldn't have just seen that. It was impossible. But the crowd behind the person didn't seem shocked at all. Now that he looked at them closer, he realized they were bored.

"Greetings, new players!" the woman said with a too-wide smile. She was dressed in a black suit. "Welcome to the competition of a lifetime! You have been randomly selected for this special virtual reality edition of *Fortnite Battle Royale*. I am the Admin and will be facilitating your tutorial."

Grey didn't know what to make of this. He had never heard of a VR version of Fortnite, and last he checked, you had to have a special visor for virtual reality.

Though he couldn't deny this was the most real VR he'd ever experienced.

He tried to grab at whatever visor might be on his head. Maybe his parents had surprised him with a graduation present. But there was nothing there. He couldn't hear anything but the game or feel anything like his bed or a desk. It was like he was actually *in* the game . . .

Except that was impossible.

"I didn't download no virtual reality edition!" the old man yelled. "How do I cancel this? Computer! Quit program!"

The Admin did not stop smiling. "As I said, none of you downloaded this edition—you were selected from around the world. But don't worry, you will be able to communicate and everyone's speech will be translated into their language. I will now explain the parameters that must be met for you to leave the competition."

"This is dodgy . . ." the girl next to him said. She already had water in her eyes, but she fought it back.

The Admin continued, "It is a new season of competition in *Battle Royale*, and the five top players have been granted a return back to the real world. Thus we welcome you to this opportunity of a lifetime! You have now joined the fight for the next two-month season, and if you rank in the top five players, you will be granted passage back to the real world as well."

"You mean we're stuck here for two months?" the teenager blurted out. "I have football camp this summer! You can't kidnap us!"

"Your bodies are currently in a comatose state

outside of the game," the Admin said. "You have not been kidnapped. Your minds are just processing this reality instead of the one you came from. While this may be difficult to accept, it will be more productive to focus on the task at hand. Not what is out of your control."

"Bring it on. Life out there sucked anyway." This voice came from the person who was on the other side of the giant football player.

Grey had to lean over to see the girl, who looked to be older than a high schooler, maybe in college. She had short green hair and she smiled like she had just gotten a free lifetime pass to her favorite amusement park.

"That is the attitude of a winner," the Admin said. "Now, let's review the structure and rules. First, while you may be familiar with Fortnite's *Battle Royale* system, the structure here is slightly different. There are only one hundred of you, so you will be playing the same adversaries for this entire season. Should a person's body be eliminated while your mind is here, an immediate replacement will be acquired mid-season. But this has not occurred as of yet, so please do not be overly concerned.

"You will be allowed to form alliances of up to

four people in a squad, but you are also allowed to go it solo if you'd prefer. All combinations will be in the same game, so it's up to you to decide what works best for you."

"That's crap," the older man complained. "No way to make it solo against squads."

"We've had three players win their way back to reality solo," the Admin defended. "As for battles, everyone is expected to fight in every battle. There will be five official battles a day, and only five. You are permitted to practice here in the lobby— there is a designated practice area arranged in similar fashion to the game. You may also talk strategy, but once the official battles begin, only squads will be able to talk to each other.

"Your player ranking will be determined by the average ranking you finish in your games overall. The top five players in average rank will not necessarily always be the top five to win in battles, but they will have an overall higher number of wins or close wins. At the end of the season, those with the top five average game rankings will leave this competition, and five new players will be welcomed."

Welcomed . . . Grey didn't think that was the right word for this situation.

While he had been excited to play *Battle Royale* just an hour ago, it didn't feel so great now that he was being forced to do it. And he couldn't help thinking about how scared his parents probably were, discovering him passed out and now in some kind of coma. That was messed up. All of this was messed up.

"The rules of this version are similar," the Admin continued in her unfeeling way. Grey couldn't tell if she was a computer program, or if a person was controlling her. Either way, she felt real and yet mechanical. "You must leave the Battle Bus and find gear to defend yourself with. All the items and their uses are similar to the computer version, as is the map. The storm also functions the same way—you must stay inside the eye or take damage.

"Your appearances as new players will be randomly generated, but as you earn rank you will be rewarded with choices in your appearance and tools. This helps players know who is higher ranking within the game and thus who they need to beat in order to improve their own rank.

"And those are the basics. Any questions?" the Admin finished.

"My parents will sue you the second I tell

them about this," the football player said. "This whole thing is messed up."

"They have to believe your claims that your consciousness spent all this time in a video game first," the Admin replied. "Our winners have yet to convince anyone of this truth."

"Why are you doing this?" the black-haired girl next to him asked quietly.

"It is an experiment on multiple levels," the Admin said. "To test the technology, to observe human behavior under stress."

"It's unethical is what it is," the old man grumbled.

"Perhaps," the Admin said. "And yet your opinions will not allow you to escape."

"Can you all stop whining?" the green-haired girl said. "Well, minus the silent kid. Let's get to the fighting!"

"Grey," the Admin said. "Hazel is right that you have not spoken. Is there anything you would like to add before we begin today's battles?"

Grey felt all eyes on him. There were so many thoughts rushing through his mind it was hard to make any of them into words. He finally settled on, "It doesn't seem like talking to you will change anything, so I don't really see the point."

The Admin smiled, but it didn't make Grey feel better. "Then let's get to the battles. This is Day One of the season. I wish you all luck."

The Admin vanished, and a siren sounded throughout the warehouse. As the other players stood and began to talk among themselves, a deep voice announced:

Battle one begins in thirty seconds. Players, ready yourselves!

Grey panicked as the words sank in. He had no time to prepare for his first battle. Finn wouldn't be there to help him out. He'd have to go it alone, and he would be on the actual island instead of looking at it on the screen.

"Ready to be eliminated, noobs?" someone called out from the crowd of people. Several people laughed.

"I'll get you first!" Hazel replied.

He didn't answer. No reason to put a target on his back when he was already a noob. All he could do was take a deep breath and hope he didn't get eliminated first.

CHAPTER 3

Grey knew all about the bright blue Battle Bus that flew over the island, but he never imagined actually *being in it* the way he was now. The hard seat, the cramped quarters, the wind as the back hatch opened. It was then that he realized he'd have to jump out of this bus and skydive. And it wouldn't just be "in a game," but it would probably feel like skydiving.

He'd never liked the feeling of falling.

While everything seemed real, some parts betrayed that it wasn't. Like the minimap on the right side of his vision, accompanied by empty squares where he'd seen Finn's inventory items go when he got them in the game. There was also a green bar that indicated his health, and one for his shield he had yet to fill. He knew he needed to find a shield item first before that would fill up and turn blue.

No one looked like they did in the lobby—like they would have in real life—now they were all designed and dressed like they belonged in *Battle Royale*. Some people had strange outfits like dinosaur hats or a superhero outfit, and many had different backpacks. He'd seen "skins" when he watched Finn play, but they weren't tied to ranking like the Admin said.

He had to admit he wanted the cool skins.

They must have earned them from their ranks in previous seasons, because he didn't see a way for him to change his appearance. He wore only the default outfit of a tank top and camo pants. His character was male, with skin three shades darker than his usual tan. He felt a lot taller and his arms looked buff.

As scared as Grey was, a spark of excitement lit inside him as well. Maybe this wouldn't be so bad. He'd be playing a game. It wasn't as if he would die in real life. If he worked hard enough, maybe he could win top five before the end of the season and be back home before he even started junior high.

He had to hope that, because the Battle Bus opened and people began to jump out. Some waited, and Grey was among them because he realized he hadn't even considered where on the map he should go. He'd seen places on Finn's computer screen, but he didn't really know where they were on the map.

Some places would be instant death for him because lots of people liked to land there. Other areas would be less populated, but they also didn't have very good items to loot.

Grey had no delusions of winning his first game—not against ninety-nine other people—but he really didn't want to be the first one eliminated.

He decided a more remote place would be the best for his first game. Not that he knew exactly what location would be remote, but he could observe where the remaining people jumped if he waited a little bit longer.

They were over the middle of the map now, and about ten people remained on the Battle Bus. Only one of them was dressed in the boring camo pants and tank top that he was, which was when he realized he'd made a mistake. Everyone else had cool outfits and backpacks. He didn't know which meant a higher rank than the other, but he could feel the players looking at him and the other new player.

They were waiting for Grey to jump . . . so they could follow him and eliminate him right off the bat.

There were two "noobs" left and eight remaining players—enough for two squads of four. He began to think this was planned. Maybe each new player had a group like this ready to kill them.

It wasn't fair.

In the normal game, it wasn't so obvious who was new and who was a pro. There were millions of people playing and you'd rarely be pitted against the same people. But in this world, his clothing made it clear. If all these other people wanted to get home, too, of course they would punish the new people.

Grey didn't have time to wait any longer. He had to jump before it would be totally obvious where he planned to land. He ran for the open hatch—hearing several pairs of footsteps behind him—and leapt out with the hopes that his glider would deploy automatically like it did for Finn. The glider would help direct his movements closer to the ground.

As he looked back, he saw four people in the sky above him. Chances were, they'd eliminate him immediately, but he had to try if he wanted to get back home.

Maybe if he found a good weapon first, he had a chance.

When Grey's glider activated, he let out a sigh of relief at the slower rate of falling. His map told him he was somewhere between Salty Springs and Fatal Fields, and he tried to focus on that instead of the people behind him. He needed a weapon, a shield, bandages—then maybe he could defend himself with some luck.

Finn always liked Fatal Fields, so Grey figured he had a decent chance there. He'd seen the layout of the farm at least, even if he hadn't played in it himself. He knew there were a lot of chests there, though it could be risky because the buildings offered tight fighting quarters where he could easily be trapped.

His glider made his movement easier to control. He pushed for the long gray barn, hoping he could get there first and find a good chest to break open.

He ran as fast as he could once he landed on the dirt, and his footsteps sounded too loud. He didn't have time to be sneaky, though, not yet. Those other players would be here, coming right for him or grabbing loot to eliminate him with. Everyone was given a pickaxe as default to break down materials for building, and he had seen people fight using the pickaxe as a weapon, but it didn't do much damage.

Inside the barn was darker than outside, and his eyes struggled to adjust to the change. There were stalls in the building, as if it housed horses, and he remembered Finn finding items here.

Sure enough, there was a treasure box in one of the stalls and he opened it. Several things burst out of it, and he grabbed the first gun he saw. It was a pistol. Not good. But there was a shield, and he used it immediately to give himself more protection. And there was ammo, too, so he figured he was better off than when he had no weapon at all. He'd just have to find something else to use in addition. There had to be more in this barn.

That's when he heard it—gunfire.

The flash of a bullet grazed by him, and he ducked down as he searched for the player. He only had nine ammo. Pistol ammo. Which wouldn't do enough damage to eliminate someone with a shield.

There was no way he would kill them, so he did the only thing he could think to do. He used his pickaxe to beat at the nearby wall. It gave him wood to build with, but it would also give him an escape route.

He busted the wall as several shots hit him and burned down his shield. Whatever weapon that player had, it was a lot better than what Grey had found.

Grey ducked behind the nearest tree, but he could tell already that it was too late for him. The shots kept coming, and then he saw another player appear from the other side. His health dwindled, and soon his vision went gray. Words appeared as he froze in his position:

Ben eliminated you.

Just as Grey feared, he was the first one to go down. Maybe it wouldn't be so easy to get home after all.

CHAPTER 4

Grey had to wait and watch until the first battle was over. It was so embarrassing. He wasn't sure what happened between the fights, but he had a feeling the players talked and someone would definitely make fun of him. Probably a lot of people.

But he tried not to feel so bad because watching the other players might help him—and he had the option to do that while eliminated from the battle. He didn't know who was good or who wasn't, so he decided he'd watch the guy who killed him, "Ben." The guy had one in his squad, someone named Tristan. Ben had decent aim and got one more elimination, but he was eliminated ranked at number 71. After that, Grey wasn't sure who to watch, but he immediately thought of Hazel, the confident new player.

May as well, though she's probably eliminated already.

The player list came back up in his vision— just thinking of her name had brought up her feed to select. So he did, and to his surprise, Hazel was still alive. There were only forty people left at this point. So she was actually good, not just talk. Maybe she could get back this season.

But she didn't last much longer. When the storm grew smaller, she was in a bad position and barely made it back inside. While she was bandaging, someone discovered her, and elimination was unavoidable.

She was the last of the people he knew, so Grey jumped through various feeds to watch the top players. It didn't make him feel great about his chances. These players knew how to build fast and they all had pinpoint aim. They were clearly on another level from him, and it seemed impossible to get that good in just one season. Especially when these people had much more practice.

He needed help. But who would help the player who was ranked 100 after the first game?

Once there were only ten players left and the storm encompassed a small portion of the map, the battle didn't last much longer. Everyone was forced to be close. The fights were fast and furious, and Grey struggled to keep up with what was happening. Finn wasn't this good. Grey had seen videos online of players like this who could build and strategize faster than he could blink, but his parents hated when he watched that, and they usually made him turn it off the second they saw it.

Someone named Tae Min took the number 1 ranking for the game. The player wore an armored suit and danced out his or her victory, but Grey had no idea who the person was among all the people he'd seen in the warehouse when he arrived.

Grey's vision went black, and he was suddenly back in that warehouse with everyone else, right where he was standing when the battle started.

One hour until the next Battle Royale! the deep voice called over the speakers. A big timer lit up on a nearby wall, ticking down the seconds until he'd have to do that all over again.

Right next to the timer was a list of all the players' names, ranked for the first game. Grey looked away, knowing exactly where he was on it.

Some people talked among their groups, what Grey guessed were squads in the game. Others argued. Many people headed outside the warehouse; to where, Grey didn't know. Several people approached the new players, but the majority came up to Hazel.

"You have some serious skills, girl," a woman who looked to be Grey's mom's age said. "We have an opening on our squad, what do you think about joining us?"

"What are your names?" Hazel said with a satisfied grin. "I want to check your rank before I commit to anything."

"Hey! I need a group! I was rank 78," the older man said.

"Me, too!" the football player chimed in. "I finished at 59! That's not bad for my first time!"

Grey backed up. It would be pointless to ask for a group with his name at the bottom of the list. As he did, he bumped into someone. "Oh, sorry . . ."

It was the new girl with the long ponytail. She began to walk away, and she looked like she was about to cry. "Don't worry about it."

She must have ranked badly, too. He looked at the rankings board, and just above him was someone named Kiri. That could have been a girl's name. Maybe it was her. "You get a bad rank, too? Are you Kiri?"

She glared at him, then turned and kept walking.

He decided to follow. Because maybe they wouldn't be the best team ever, but it had to be better than nothing. "I'm not trying to make fun of you! I'm dead last!"

"Go away!" the girl yelled.

They left the warehouse, and to his surprise there was a vast space outside that looked a lot like the game. There were buildings and hills, trees and brush to hide behind. The nearest structures looked like they might be cabins to stay in, as several people stood outside them. There was also a large clearing and another warehouse, but this one looked like it was set up for practicing.

Kiri didn't stop walking, but sped up to a run once they got outside.

"Hey wait!" he called out.

"Just leave me alone!" she yelled as she ran into the woodsy area by the cabins. "I don't want to talk to you!"

He stopped walking. She obviously didn't want help, and it wasn't like he had much time to convince her before the next battle. He'd have to change his plans if even the second-worst player wouldn't team up with him.

Maybe it was better to check out the practice area.

Because even if he was rank 100, he wasn't about to give up. Sometimes games were unlucky, and he might do better next time. Maybe if he got a decent rank next game, people would see that he could improve at least.

Sure enough, when he got to the other warehouse, words popped up in his vision: *Activating Practice Mode.* The inventory slots from *Battle Royale* appeared at the right side of his vision, as well as those for materials. He could pull out a pickaxe when he couldn't before. Several people had items from inside the game. They shot at each other, but no one seemed to be taking damage. He didn't see a shield or health meter like in the game, so they must have been disabled in practice. The other players built structures and ran around them, freely talking about what might be a good spot to stand in or how to aim with their weapons.

As he walked by, they would stop talking and stare at him. They must not have wanted him to hear their strategies. So much for learning from others. People appeared to be in their chosen squads, and he felt left out once again.

But Grey wouldn't let that stop him. He marched into the warehouse, where there were items lined up on the walls for the taking. He grabbed a rifle—how he wished he'd gotten that instead of a pistol in the first game. There was no ammo, but the gun showed an infinity sign next to it. Practice weapons must not have had the restrictions they had in the game. He decided to take a few others to test out. The least he could do was work on his aim.

"Hey, 100," a boy's voice said.

Grey turned around, finding a blond-haired boy with a confident grin. He had a feeling this wouldn't be a nice conversation. "Hey?"

"It's me, Ben," the boy said with a laugh. "I got you first."

"Oh." Grey didn't know what to say, but his face felt hot.

"Don't worry too much—no one stays 100 for more than a game," Ben continued. "Averages, you know? How old are you?"

"Twelve," Grey said.

"Cool, I'm thirteen. And where are you from?"

"California," Grey said.

"Nice, I'm from Utah." Ben held up his rifle. "Me and my buddy Tristan are doing some hide and seek. Wanna practice with us?"

"Really?" Grey could hardly believe it, since this was the guy who killed him without mercy in the game. "That'd be awesome."

"Let's go find him, then. He's had more than enough time to get in position." Ben headed outside the practice warehouse, and Grey followed closely behind. Now that death wasn't imminent, he realized running didn't make him winded. So this wasn't his real body, even if it felt like it. There didn't seem to be pain, either. At least that was nice. "The practice zone is this whole area, plus those hills and the ghost town that way. If you go outside it, your items disappear and you can't get hit."

"Got it." Grey searched over the area, noting there were several obstacles that mimicked the game. Rocks and trees to be broken down for materials, huts and buildings to use as cover.

"Bet he's at the ghost town," Ben said. "Tristan likes tight-quarters fighting, even if he's not great at it."

"Why would he like it if he's bad at it?" Grey asked.

"More exciting." Ben slowed his pace as they approached the most predictable version of an Old West ghost town possible. It was a long street with tattered wood buildings on both sides. Grey half expected the tumbleweeds to blow in the wind, but they stayed in place. He realized there wouldn't be a breeze in a video game. They crouched behind a batch of hay bales. "By the way, Tristan is a bit cranky. Don't let it get to you."

"Cranky?" Grey repeated.

Ben shrugged. "Yeah, not friendly? But he's not a bad guy. He's from Germany—I don't think the translator helps. He's just really . . . honest. He might be cranky that I brought you, but he'll be fine. He's just upset we didn't get home in the last season. Again."

This warning did not make Grey feel good about agreeing to this, as much as he wanted to learn from other players. "Should I go back?"

"Oh, no! Stay," Ben said. "Back me up, okay?"

"I'll try . . ."

Ben stepped out and ran for what looked like a saloon, with the swinging doors and everything. Grey followed right behind, and a few shots broke the windows and hit Ben. He didn't falter, although his body blinked red as he took the shots. "I knew he'd be here! Change of plans—you go around back. There's a door to the kitchen. He'll never guess you're smart enough for that."

"Okay." Grey tried to ignore the slight insult because he was learning. And he needed to do as much of that as possible. While Ben shot through the swinging door and Tristan shot back, Grey jumped over the porch railing and headed to the back door.

For the first time since entering this hacked version of *Battle Royale*, Grey felt himself smile. This was a lot more fun when his rank didn't depend on it. He didn't feel like he had to be perfect. Maybe he didn't know Ben or Tristan, but he could pretend for a second that he was playing with Finn from his computer at home.

The shots Tristan and Ben exchanged drowned out the sound of Grey's footsteps. He opened the back door and raised the gun he'd chosen. It was a "scar," one of the best. Grey peeked around the kitchen corner. There was a boy with sandy blond hair who was very tall and skinny. Grey assumed this was Tristan, who was shooting from the staircase and didn't even see him.

Grey had the perfect shot, so he took it.

The boy was startled, and his eyes immediately went to Grey's position. "What the—?"

Ben burst in from the front of the saloon, laughing hard. "Got you! I brought backup this time. This is Grey."

"Rank 100?" Tristan gave Grey a skeptical look. "Why'd you bring him? He was awful."

So there was the cranky honesty Ben warned Grey about.

"He came right to the practice area after the game." Ben shrugged. "I dunno, shows determination at least. I think he's got potential if he's willing to work hard."

Tristan sighed. "We can't keep picking up scrubs, Ben. We need a *better* squad."

"Well, they won't recruit us!" Ben replied. "And it's better to be grouped anyway. He took my directions perfectly."

"He'll leave us like the rest have." Tristan glared at Grey. "He'll get a few skills and some other group will recruit him like always. Unless you just want to stay in here forever, ranked in the seventies and sixties."

"You're so negative," Ben grumbled. "I'm just trying to help us."

Grey realized this might be his only chance to have a group, and he wasn't about to let it pass by. "I won't leave you. I promise. Why would I leave?"

"That promise will mean nothing when a top squad has an open spot." Tristan leaned on the stair railing. "We'd all betray each other for a chance to escape."

"C'mon, Tris," Ben said. "Even after all this time?"

"Wouldn't even feel bad," he replied.

Ben looked hurt, but he tried to push it back. "Well, you won't get recruited if we don't have a full squad. We need teamwork to boost our ranks—neither of us is a soloer. Can't we just give him a chance? Like you said, nothing is permanent."

"Fine, a chance," Tristan said as he headed for the saloon's front exit. "Let's go, next battle will be starting soon."

"That's the spirit!" Ben gave Grey a big smile. "I swear he's nicer than he looks—he's just been here for a long time without much progress. Some days, he thinks he'll never get out."

"How long?" Grey asked as he made his way across the room to leave with Ben.

"Since the beginning. Five whole seasons." Ben walked with him while Tristan stayed several paces ahead.

"Ten months? That sucks." Grey could hardly believe it . . . and Tristan would be here another two months at least. A full year of his life. Stuck in a video game.

"It's not so bad," Ben said, although his smile wasn't as bright as it had just been. "No homework. Or parents yelling at you. Or chores. I mean, I've missed all of seventh grade at this point, but I hear it's overrated."

"Yeah . . ." Grey felt a chill run up his spine. So Ben had been here that long, too. Would Grey spend the next year of his life in *Battle Royale*? Not that he knew the exact odds of getting out, but they felt a lot smaller all of the sudden.

Next Battle Royale in one minute! The deep voice sounded throughout the area.

"Ready to boost that rank?" Ben asked.

Grey nodded. "So ready."

The seconds ticked down, and even though

they were nowhere near the warehouse Grey had first landed in, his vision grew dark and he prepared for what he'd see next—the blue Battle Bus and the island that held his fate.

CHAPTER 5

Maybe Ben and Tristan were ranked only in the seventies after the first battle, but Grey was more than happy to have them on his side for this game. Unlike the all-anonymous players of last battle, this time "Ben" and "Tristan" hovered above two players nearby. They were both girl avatars in standard garb like him, but they had backpacks that were striped. That must have been one of the rank indicators.

"Let's go Salty Springs," Tristan said.

"Should be enough loot for all of us there," Ben said. "Just follow behind us, Grey. Play backup like in practice."

"Got it." Grey was determined to make a

good impression this time. Surely he wouldn't be last in rank with these guys on his squad.

"Oh, and it's squad rule that I deal out the items," Tristan said. "So the good stuff isn't wasted on new players like you."

"Okay, makes sense." Grey tried to remember how Ben said Tristan always sounded cranky. He wasn't wrong so far. Grey would just have to take what he was given, but surely it would be better than the pistol he got last game.

"Jumping . . . now!" Tristan leapt from the plane. Ben and Grey followed right behind. They were high above the island, and the only way that Grey could tell where they were was the mini-map. It said they were soaring over a crater called Dusty Divot—he recalled that was a place for tough fights, according to Finn. They released their gliders, and this was when Grey got to see that Ben and Tristan had also earned an umbrella-style glider instead of the default one he had.

That meant they had gotten one "Victory Royale" in their time playing. At least that was what it meant in the normal game.

Salty Springs looked like a neighborhood, one of the nicer ones, with big trees and spacious houses. Grey didn't live in a place like that, but in a neighborhood with houses all squished together. He suddenly missed his home, realizing it would be a long time before he saw it, at this rate.

Instead of landing on the ground, they landed on the roof of a house, and they began to break it down to get inside. Grey felt a little stupid that he didn't think of that last game—he'd just landed on the ground. But now that he thought about it, lots of videos he had seen started like this. His friend Finn had used the tactic, too.

"Do you have any practice fighting?" Tristan asked as they fell through the broken roof and landed right on a golden chest.

"Just what we did today," Grey admitted as they opened it. "Only got to watch friends and streamers before."

"So you know some basics at least. But we can't even guess if you're good at anything." Tristan picked up the basic AR that popped out of the chest. "Can't trust you to use it well, even if it's basic. You can have it if I find better."

"That's fair," Grey had to admit, although it was annoying to hear yet again. He wanted good loot to see what he could do with it, but he understood. If Ben and Tristan had better guns with better aim than he had, they all had a higher chance of surviving longer.

"We gotta move fast," Ben said as they broke down another floor and escaped the attic. This room had ammo and bandages but no chest. "There's usually a lot of loot in this house so don't worry. Keep your eyes out for enemies."

"Okay." Grey did just that. He watched their back as the chests were opened and the loot was gathered. He got the "worst" of the gear, but he still had a rifle, pistol, and enough ammo and bandages to feel safer than in his first battle. He also had learned how to loot a house much faster—these guys had definitely memorized where and how to get to the good items.

What was even better, some players had already been eliminated somewhere on the map. That meant Grey already wasn't the first eliminated. His rank would go up.

"Look over there at that other house," Ben whispered, as if enemies could hear them. "What do you see?"

Grey peered through the windows, and for a moment he saw nothing. But then he realized there was a gap in the roof where it had been broken.

Just like they had broken in.

"Someone else is over there," Grey said.

"Exactly." Ben smiled. "Time to get some kills."

"Any visual?" Tristan asked as he used one of the traps they'd found to barricade the door. Grey knew the trap would damage anyone who tried to go through the door or break the wall.

"Not yet." Ben moved to another window, peeking out and moving back to avoid being shot or spotted himself. "Grey, check the other one over there."

"Okay." Grey moved to the window at the back of the living room where they had just finished looting the house. There were two windows, and he mimicked what Ben did to check for enemy players. Motion caught his eye. His heart raced faster and he ducked back behind the wall. "One back here! Maybe more."

"Did they see you?" Tristan asked.

"Don't think so."

"Then take a shot!"

"Right." Grey lifted his weapon and took a deep breath to steady himself. He peeked back outside the window and spotted the player hacking at a tree for materials. The player didn't seem to be in a group after all. He raised his rifle and pulled the trigger.

Numbers appeared above the player, first blue to show shield damage and then white for damage to the character.

Before he knew it, the player fell to the ground and their loot burst out of them.

You eliminated Kiri.

Grey could hardly believe it, but he had just eliminated his first player. He felt bad that it happened to be the girl just above him in the ranks, and yet that was how it had to be. She hadn't been eliminated first that battle either, so at least they had both done better than before.

"Nice, dude!" Ben said as he came up behind Grey. "Let's see what she had."

They moved outside and looked over Kiri's loot. It made Grey feel bad, but she had a really nice gun that he picked up. "I can have this right? Since I got the kill?"

Tristan took it himself. "No, I get it. You can have the basic AR. We can't waste this ammo— there isn't much."

Grey wanted to argue, but there wasn't time. He took what Tristan gave, since it was still better than what he had and there was plenty of ammo for it.

"We'll have to find more," Ben said. "Hurry, let's loot the rest of this place and get some mats before this storm shrinks."

"We're in a bad position," Tristan said. "It'll be dangerous to get to the safe zone."

Grey looked at the minimap, and sure enough, the indicated zone for the next storm was much further away from them than he'd like. If they got caught in it, they would take damage until they got to a safe area. Maybe they wouldn't get eliminated right away, but it would leave them weak and vulnerable.

Grey beat down some walls with his new squad, and wood filled his supply slot. He'd never actually built anything, but he knew how important it was to learn how to build well. If you could make a structure fast, you often had the upper hand on your opponents. They also ran through the rest of the houses at Salty Springs, encountering another solo player who almost downed Tristan. Ben eliminated the enemy in time, though, and Tristan used a "chug jug" to fill his shield and life to full.

Before Grey knew it, there were only sixty players left alive on the map. It was a big difference from his last battle, and he was glad this would improve his average.

But the storm timer still counted down, and it felt like maybe they should get going. "How much loot do we need?"

"As much as possible," Tristan said.

"Retail Row isn't that far, but we need loot and mats because there are probably people there already," Ben said.

"Right." Grey wouldn't say it out loud, but he was afraid of being caught in the storm. It seemed like a pretty embarrassing way to be eliminated, seeing as all you had to do was pay attention and not be in it.

They had one minute to get to the safe zone.

It didn't feel like enough time, and as they left Salty Springs and headed for the outskirts of Retail Row, the purple haze of the storm came upon them. Grey began to panic as he took damage, even though it was only one tick of health at a time. All their health dwindled as they ran, which would have been bad enough, but then Grey heard shots fired.

"Ugh!" Ben had taken a lot of damage from

the storm, and now he'd lost his shield due to the enemies shooting at them. They tried to take cover, but Ben fell to the ground and could only crawl unless they tried to revive him.

Which would definitely get them all killed.

"I'm done for—hide!" Ben said as his character took another shot and was down permanently, his loot scattered all around his body.

Ben was eliminated by Sandhya.

Grey and Tristan were still in the storm, and the enemies fired on them from the safe zone. They ducked behind a small hill, and Tristan built a ramp for them to get up a safer way and out of the storm.

But it was too late.

The other players had their location and they shot at them relentlessly. Grey fired back like Tristan did, but the shots they landed weren't enough when they both had such low health from the storm. Grey went down, and Tristan right after.

Hazel eliminated Grey.

Hazel eliminated Tristan.

Their loot spilled from their bodies, and the victors did a dance before they took what they wanted and moved on. So Hazel was doing as well in this second game as she had in the first. And clearly she had joined someone's squad.

Grey could only hope he'd someday get payback.

CHAPTER 6

Though Grey was eliminated, it felt a lot better to be at rank 57 for that battle, rather than at 100 like last time. And, what was cooler, a screen popped up in his vision showing him what rewards he'd been given for his new average ranking. With an average rank of 78, he had earned a checkered backpack and blue color for his avatar's glider. They weren't as cool as the ones that Ben and Tristan had, but it was something.

Grey appeared in the same place he had been when the battle started—in the practice area with Ben beside him. Nothing had changed about the area around them. The sun was still in the same position, as were the clouds. The only change he could see was that the things people had built in the practice area were gone. The area must have reset between each battle.

Ben had a big grin on his face. "See? We did better together!"

"Yeah." Grey smiled, too. "That was fun."

Tristan was still walking ahead of them, and he didn't come back to comment. Instead, he kept walking back to the practice warehouse.

"Your average rank probably jumped a lot, right? Get any skins?" Ben asked.

"A backpack and a glider color," Grey said. He couldn't wait to try them out in the next game.

"Cool. You also get them when you stay in the same ranking average for a certain number of games," Ben said. "Like, if you're ranked between 50 and 60 for twenty games, you get new stuff."

"Nice." It wouldn't be easy, but Grey didn't feel nearly as hopeless about getting home this season as he had after the first game. And he wanted to help Ben and Tristan rank up, too. They had been here so long and deserved to go home. They were nice enough to help him out instead of helping themselves.

"What's the highest you've ever been ranked?" Grey asked.

Ben didn't look too happy about it when he said, "Yeah, I've never gotten much higher than a 50 average. But it's really hard. We've won games before—we're not, like, that bad—it's just you have to *always* get close to winning to get a high average and that's nearly impossible. Except for Tae Min. That guy . . . is a god. No one can keep up with him."

"Tae Min?" Grey hadn't looked closely at the leader board last time he was by it, only at his own rank and a couple others. But the name was familiar. Grey was pretty sure that was the person who eliminated Hazel in the first game.

"Yeah, he's a weird dude. He's been here since the beginning, like me and Tristan, and he gets a ton of Victory Royales and is always the top player for most of the season." Ben and Grey had arrived back at the practice warehouse, and Ben swapped out new weapons to practice with. "But right at the end, he takes a bunch of losses on purpose—like rank 100 losses—and he ends up not being in the top five. He could have gone home every season, but it's like he doesn't want to."

"Why not?" Grey couldn't imagine wanting to stay in here for a year. While playing a few games in real virtual reality had been cool, he already missed his home and friends. He also hadn't seen any food, and it felt like he would be missing that soon, too.

"No one knows. Tae Min sticks to himself." Ben looked over the wall of weapons, his usual high energy waning. "People try to talk to him once they figure out he's so good. They ask him to be in a squad, but he always turns everyone down and does it on his own. Me and Tristan asked him way back in our first season, but he said he didn't need people holding him back. That was the last time I asked, though Tristan has a few more times."

"Holding him back?" Grey thought that sounded overly confident. "So he's kind of a jerk."

"Yeah, I guess." Ben let out a long sigh and ended up putting all his weapons back. "But I don't know for sure. He's not like the people here who make fun of others or trash-talk a lot. Or the people who brag all the time, even though he is better than all of them. He's just quiet. And every time he tanks his own score . . ."

"What?" Grey insisted when he realized Ben wasn't going to finish his sentence.

"Someone you would never think would

make it to the top five starts winning every battle and they shoot up." Ben shrugged. "I can't
prove it, but it's sorta like Tae Min picks a person
to take his spot. Someone he thinks deserves it,
though they could never get it on their own. I
don't know how he teaches them to win so fast,
but I swear he does. So I can't really call him a
jerk, though maybe he is. He's just Tae Min."

Grey nodded. He didn't know what to make
of this new information, but he did know he
wasn't just a noob in *Battle Royale*.

He was a noob in this virtual world, too. And
that seemed just as dangerous.

With only one hundred players always fighting against each other and no one else, things
were bound to get complicated outside the battles as well. A lot of these people probably had
history with each other. Rivalries. Alliances.
Friendships. He thought about how the Admin
had said this was a "social experiment." Grey was
starting to see just how true that was.

He also wished Tae Min would pick him.
How lucky would that be? If the top player for
five seasons helped him, that would be the sur-
est way to get out. But it didn't sound like Grey
could convince Tae Min . . . it sounded like Tae

Min was the one who chose, and no one knew the criteria.

"Okay, enough drama!" Ben declared. "Just how much did you play before you got sucked into the game?"

"It was literally my first time logging on," Grey admitted. "I've watched my buddy Finn play, but my parents wouldn't let me until the end of the school year."

"Gotcha. Well, you have decent aim, that's a good natural skill. Let's work on trap strategies before the next battle. It can be handy in tight places like those Salty Springs houses." Ben stood up and grabbed some traps.

Grey did, too. "Sounds good. Where's Tristan?"

"Probably sulking. Or asking to be in a new squad," Ben said. "He does that a lot."

This surprised Grey. "That doesn't bother you?"

Ben paused before he answered. "A little, but it's not personal. He really wants to get out. I think he misses Germany a lot more than he'll ever say out loud. He actually wasn't much of a gamer—he was a competitive rock climber."

"Really?" Grey couldn't picture it, but it was

hard to imagine what any of the players did out-side the game.

Ben nodded. "He told me one night early on, when he was really homesick. He said he was going to miss the juvenile championship or something, and he was supposed to win."

"That sucks." Grey suddenly felt bad for Tristan, even if he hadn't been very nice so far. Grey's life was pretty average—it would be hor-rible to miss something cool like that.

"Yeah," Ben said. "So sometimes he tries to get in a better group, but squads only recruit when they feel like it, not when others ask. Tristan comes off desperate . . . he is, and he always comes back without a new squad."

Grey didn't know what to say to that.

"He's not a bad guy, either," Ben went on. "You gotta realize everyone here wants out. Except maybe Tae Min. We try to be friends, but in the end we're all fighting each other, you know? I can't be mad at Tris for wanting to find a better chance at leaving. Sometimes it makes me feel like crap, but I get it."

"Why don't you try to get in a better squad like he does?" Grey asked.

"We just have different ways of thinking."

Ben handed Grey a bunch of traps. "You see, I figure if I practice my butt off and get to be an amazing player, then people will come to me asking me to join them. Maybe I'm just not good enough yet, you know? Tris thinks we're good enough, but that people are sabotaging us. He tries to work the system. In the end, it's probably somewhere in the middle. But this is the best I can do, you know?"

Grey thought about this for a moment. "I guess I think more like you. I need a lot of practice, and then I'll get better and win."

Ben smiled. "See? I knew that the moment you showed up here. Lots of people think it's all luck and not practice, so they don't come here at all. But let's prove them wrong, okay?"

"Yeah, totally."

And so they practiced laying traps. Ben showed Grey how, if he looked closely, he could see the borders on the wall or floor. He said enemy traps glowed yellow and friendly ones glowed blue. Lots of new players wouldn't pay attention, but it could save Grey's life and ranks. He was glad to learn, because he'd never noticed that about traps before.

Then they played the rest of the games for

the day. They didn't do better than that second game, but they didn't do terribly, either. Tristan got the most eliminations of everyone and actually had precise aim. He could also build faster than Grey could even think. Grey could tell Tristan had been working hard to get home.

After the fifth and final game of the day, Grey appeared in the main warehouse with the rest of the players. It was odd because he was in a line, not next to Ben or Tristan, but next to people he didn't know.

No one moved, so he figured he should stay there.

The Admin appeared. "First day battles have ended, and these are your final rankings for the day. Please also see the board for your sleeping quarters assignments, which will be permanent for the season. To maintain fairness, all persons are expected to be in bed at ten and to rise at eight. Anyone found outside their cabins after ten will be penalized by losing rank. Other than that, you are free to mingle and practice until then."

Once the Admin vanished, everyone relaxed and began to find their squads again. Grey looked over the rankings board. After five games, he was ranked 71. Many people had average rankings that were tied, Ben and Tristan included—Grey realized these were the squads. No one had a ranking of 100 like he started with.

Tae Min was at the top, with a shocking rank of 1. Grey could hardly believe he'd beaten everyone all day. That was impossible. Even the best *Battle Royale* streamers didn't always win.

Kiri had the lowest ranking at 90. Grey spotted her looking at the sleeping assignments. Instead of crying like before, she had cinched her brows together in anger. He couldn't tell if it was a show or not, but he still felt bad for her. They had an open spot in their squad, and he wished he could ask her to join them. If he could improve so fast with a little help, he thought Kiri could, too.

He didn't think Tristan would go for it, since he barely let Grey in.

But Grey couldn't shake the thought. He just had a feeling people were counting Kiri out before she even had a fair chance. He really wanted to give her one, like Ben had given him one.

Grey glanced at his sleeping arrangements next. He was happy to see Ben and Tristan in his cabin and was surprised to see Tae Min in there as well. The fifth roommate was someone named Lorenzo he didn't know yet.

"Are you serious?" It was Ben's voice, and when he turned he saw Ben with Tristan. They didn't seem happy.

"You know I can't refuse their offer," Tristan said. "They always rank in the forties at least, usually thirties."

It sounded like Tristan really had gotten recruited by a higher-ranked squad this time.

"Yeah, I know." Ben looked hurt, though he'd talked about how he understood. He took a deep breath and said, "Good luck, I guess."

"You, too," Tristan said with the smallest hint of remorse. "You deserve better."

As Tristan walked away from Ben, Grey felt bad but also relieved. He'd have a much easier time convincing Ben that they should add Kiri to their squad.

Now he'd just have talk to her and see if she'd join.

CHAPTER 7

Grey had several hours before their mandatory bedtime, so he went over to Ben and immediately started in. "Sorry about Tristan."

Ben nodded. "Like I said, it was bound to happen. His new squad was one of the better ones last season, and their top guy got sent home at the end. They only had one spot open. He's lucky."

It seemed like Ben wished he was lucky, too. "Would you have gone to that squad if they had two openings?"

Ben didn't answer.

Grey figured that meant Ben probably would have left him alone if he got an offer. They needed a topic change, so Grey sucked in a breath and gathered his courage to ask, "So, I was thinking of asking Kiri to practice with us, maybe join if she's not as bad as it seems."

Ben cringed. "I don't know . . . she seems like a scaredy-cat."

"Maybe she's totally new, kinda like me," Grey offered.

Ben took a moment to answer, but then said, "I guess it wouldn't hurt to offer a practice session. If you can get her to say yes. She's got loner status written all over her."

"I'll meet you over there," Grey said. It didn't seem like there would be anything to eat, and he hadn't felt hungry or the need to go to the bathroom, so he figured practice was about all they could do. Although even if he wasn't hungry, he wished there was food. He always looked forward to meals.

Many more people now began to head toward the practice area than had gone there during the battles. But Kiri lingered at a table away from everyone else. Grey walked over to her, and when she noticed, she rolled her eyes. "You don't learn, do you?"

"I have learned, actually," Grey said with

confidence as he pointed to the score board. "I'm twenty ranks higher than you now."

She gave him a nasty glare for that.

"Look, I'm trying to help," Grey continued. "We just lost a squad member. It's fine if you don't want to join, but it's an offer if you want it. At least come practice with me and Ben. He's really nice and he's been here since the beginning—he knows a lot. We could all help each other out, you know?"

Kiri pursed her lips, thinking. "I reckon I better."

"Reckon?" Grey smiled at the term. The game might have translated everything from other languages or accents, but apparently not phrases. "You from Texas or something?"

"New Zealand, mate," she replied.

"Oh, wow, cool," Grey answered. He liked hearing different accents and was sad hers was gone. "Well, Ben should be waiting for us. Let's go."

"Sweet as." She got up, and as they walked Grey began to feel awkward in the silence.

"So, first time playing?" he asked when he couldn't take it anymore.

"Yeah," she said with a hint of anger. "I lost

a bet to my brother and he made me try it. He should be the one stuck here. Not me. I don't even like gaming—I like sports."

"Oh." So that explained her panic. "Well, he must have got a shock when you passed out at the computer."

Kiri smiled the littlest bit. "Didn't think of it like that. I hope he feels guilty."

"Apparently we're all in comas," Grey said. "So probably."

"Was it your first time, too?" Kiri asked him.

Grey nodded. "I'd watched some of my friends play, but never got a chance myself. I finished school today and my parents let me play because I got good grades."

"What a prize . . ."

He laughed a little. "Yeah. And hey, when you think about it, this is sort of a sport. It is a competition."

"It's not netball, but I guess that's true," she said.

"Netball?" Grey hadn't heard of a sport called netball, but maybe it was something like cricket that wasn't popular in America.

"Grey! Kiri!" Ben's voice called to them, and it took Grey a moment to spot him with all the people in the open practice space. It was chaos in comparison to earlier, with squads building large structures and fighting each other out of them. Though things looked competitive, there was laughter and people talked and it didn't seem nearly as tense as it did in the game.

"Hey, Ben, I'm guessing?" Kiri said when they got close enough.

"Yup." Ben smiled, even though before he didn't look excited to have her join them. "Thanks for joining us. Wasn't sure you would."

"I wouldn't thank me. I'm rubbish," she admitted.

"That can change," Ben said. "Let's see if we can find something you're good at. Or at least something you like. We have a few hours."

"Sure." Kiri looked at the buildings all around her. "How do they build so fast?"

"Practice." Ben motioned for them to follow to the practice warehouse to get weapons and materials. "Building is actually a massive part of how the best teams win. I wish I was better at it, but I feel like I'm average at best. Don't usually get to end game when people build a lot."

"Maybe we should focus on basics, though," Grey said. "She's never played at all or even watched."

"Right. Cool." Ben grabbed some guns off the wall for himself. "Then what's the hardest part so far, Kiri?"

Kiri picked at the ends of her long, thick hair. "Everything? I see a person in the battles and I just . . . panic. They're shooting me before I can even think to shoot back. Then I'm eliminated."

"Okay then, shooting practice it is!" Ben said. "We can get away from the crowds and you can practice shooting us, all right? In practice you don't get hurt or eliminated, so just unload on us until you feel better about your aim. We'll hit the ghost town again."

"I could use more dodging practice," Grey said. "This works."

"Sweet as," she said.

Armed and ready, they headed back out to the ghost town in the practice area. The sun was still in the same place, even though it was supposedly later in the "day." Grey wondered if the lighting would ever change, but he realized it didn't in Fortnite *Battle Royale*, so why would it here? The scenery was all stuck in place, nothing was really growing, there were no animals, no nights. Grey had a feeling this would get boring fast.

"So Kiri," Ben said. "You stick in the

schoolhouse, okay? We will come at you and you keep an eye out and shoot whenever you see us. Don't be afraid to miss—you won't run out of ammo. Just try to get used to people coming after you."

"Right."

"Grey, spread out and try to be sneaky," Ben said.

"Yup." Grey was ready and excited. He liked the idea of helping someone else, even if it was a competitor.

He took off running in the opposite direction of Ben, deciding he'd go out into the surrounding fields and hills. The schoolhouse was at the end of the ghost town street, and Ben ducked into the buildings for a different approach. Grey took shelter behind a big patch of rocks and counted to sixty before he decided to start heading back.

Waiting would probably stress Kiri out more, which would help emulate the game better. He imagined her searching desperately for a target. He heard no gun shots, so she hadn't spotted Ben yet, either.

Grey peeked out from the rock formation. The schoolhouse was a tiny speck of a building from this distance, but that didn't mean she wouldn't spot him. He'd seen players take amazing sniper shots at people. Kiri probably didn't know she could do that, but he wouldn't count it out.

There was a nearby patch of trees, and he decided that would be his first destination on the path back. He began running—jumping, too—in hopes of dodging potential bullets.

The sound of a shot echoed throughout the area.

To Grey's shock, his body flashed to indicate he'd been hit.

He kept going, getting hit again before he made it to the trees. His eyes grew wide as he stared at the schoolhouse. Was that Kiri? He was so far away. It couldn't possibly be her. Maybe there was someone else in the area messing around with him. He looked all around him, trying to find another culprit.

He didn't see anyone.

The next closest cover was an outhouse on the outskirts of town. This time, he determined he'd look right at the schoolhouse to make sure the bullets came from there.

Grey began to run, and sure enough, a flash of fire came from the bell tower on the schoolhouse.

He flashed again. If those shots had counted for damage, he was certain he'd be eliminated by now. One of the shots missed, and then she got him two more times before he ducked behind the outhouse.

Shots still fired, but this time there were more from inside the schoolhouse. It must have been Ben.

Grey began running for the schoolhouse, and this time no shots came his way. The fight was happening inside. As he got closer, he heard Kiri's panicked cries and yelling. "Get away! Get away! Get away!"

"I'm right in front of you!" Ben yelled back. "How can you miss from here?"

Grey ran up the stairs that led to the bell tower, and he spotted them at the other end of the building shooting at each other. Kiri had broken several walls and roof tiles in her attempts to hit Ben, who moved back and forth to avoid her attempts.

"I'm trying!" she cried back. "You scared me! How was I supposed to know you'd sneak up on me?"

"I told you that's what we'd do." Ben began to laugh.

And then Kiri stopped shooting and started laughing, too. "I know, and I still panicked. See? I'm absolute rubbish."

Ben cringed. "I hate to say it, but—"

"No you're not," Grey said.

Kiri squeaked in surprised, neither of them having noticed he was there yet. "Don't do that!"

"Sorry." Grey came closer, excitement coursing through him. He turned to Ben. "Dude, she hit me like five times from sniper position."

Ben looked confused. "What?"

Grey pointed out the opening in the bell tower. "I went all the way out there to that rock formation. How far you think that is from here?"

"Like at least three hundred yards," Ben said. He grabbed his sniper gun and held it up. "Two hundred and seventy-two, to be exact."

"Well, she hit me several times," Grey said.

"It's easier to hit someone when I have time to aim," Kiri explained. "And they're not right in my face scaring me. You didn't even notice me."

"That usually makes it harder, being so far," Grey said. "I'd have been eliminated. Ben, do you think she's, like, some natural sniper or something?"

Ben raised an eyebrow. "I don't know, but we should try it out. No offense, but it's one thing for her to be able to hit you, and a different story if she can hit me."

"None taken," Grey said. He handed Kiri his better sniper gun. "Here, try this one, too."

"Okay . . ." Kiri didn't seem to believe in her own skills, but if Grey was right, they'd just found an amazing ally. Not everyone could snipe well. Most of the time they were just lucky shots. If Kiri had more than just luck, they might be able to do really well in the ranks.

"Let's build a taller structure and see what she can do," Ben said. "C'mon."

They followed Ben to the hill where Grey had hidden behind the rocks and built a tower much taller than the schoolhouse. Kiri sat atop it and smiled. "I do feel much safer like this. I need to learn to build towers. Much better than being out in the open."

"If you know how to use them to your advantage," Ben said. "Gotta be careful if enemies bust it down. You can fall and die."

"Good to know." Kiri kneeled down and put her eye to the scope. "What now?"

"Well, we disappear, and you try to hit us if you see us." Ben was already heading down the ramp. "I'm a lot harder target than Grey."

"You think you're pretty flash, ay?" Kiri said.

"Flash? Uh, sure. Now focus!" Ben continued on his path, and Grey followed behind him as the ramp wound down the structure. Once they were further away from Kiri, Ben whispered, "If she's a good sniper, we are so lucky. I might understand why Tristan left, but I still want to make him regret it."

"I'll do my best," Grey said. "Maybe if she's good at sniping, I can focus on learning how to build."

"Yeah, totally. That'd be perfect." They stood at the bottom of the tower, and Ben looked hopeful as he thought things over. "Okay, you head over there, and I'll go the opposite. That way, we can see how she handles being surrounded."

"Aye, aye, Captain."

Grey ran off in his assigned direction and into a thick patch of trees. Last time he had waited a minute, but this time he decided to wait much longer. It wasn't as if they were running out of time. He guessed they still had over an hour to practice before they had to be in their cabins. He didn't know a lot about snipers, but he imagined there was patience involved. He didn't think he could do it—he'd get too antsy and want to come down and find people to eliminate. Or he'd be afraid of someone else sniping him while he stayed in one place for so long.

It seemed Ben was taking the same approach as Grey, because the surrounding area was silent. There were gunshots in the distance, where everyone was trying their builds by the practice warehouse, but other than that, there was nothing to hear but his own breathing.

The nature around him didn't make noise unless he interacted with it, and he had never realized just how noisy the real world was when he stepped outside his door in the morning. Traffic sounds. Wind in the trees. Birds chirping. There was nothing like that, only his breathing and footsteps when he moved or the sound effects of breaking stuff or shooting.

After what he thought was five minutes, Grey began to move through the trees back to Kiri. There was a small clearing, and he was curious to see if she had her sharp eye on him at all, so he sprinted across the middle of it instead of skirting around the edge.

He got shot.

And grinned about it.

He must have been at least two hundred

yards away still. That girl had to have binocu-
lars for eyes to spot movement so far off. The
scope might have helped her aim, but a person
still needed to know where to point first.

Another shot sounded, but Grey didn't see
any flash of bullets this time. Kiri must have
found Ben, too. Grey hoped she hit him on the
first shot so he'd stop saying he was better at
dodging—all dodging seemed like luck at this
distance. Several more shots followed, but none
were directed at Grey.

Once he reached the edge of the forest, Kiri
found him again and didn't let up with her end-
less supply of ammo. She'd finally realized she
could take down obstacles if she kept shooting,
and the trees broke down as she kept her focus on
Grey. He got hit several times, though he couldn't
tell for how much damage or if they were "head
shots," which did the most damage and were the
hardest to aim.

He and Ben finally made it back into the
tower. As they climbed the ramps to meet Kiri,
Ben couldn't stop laughing.

"How'd I do?" Kiri said with a wide grin.

"I think you know already," Ben replied.

"Please, please join our squad. We'll protect you while you snipe everyone down."

"You'll make everyone regret counting you out," Grey added, hoping she would join.

Kiri looked away from them, her face growing serious. "Why didn't you count me out, Grey?"

Grey's words got stuck in his throat. It felt like saying the wrong thing might ruin their chance. He took a deep breath and went for honesty. "Well, everyone deserves a chance, don't they? Just because someone is new at something doesn't mean they won't eventually be the best. We all start at the beginning. There's no reason to be embarrassed by that."

Kiri nodded. "Okay, I'm in. Let's make them all regret overlooking us."

Ben pumped his fists, and Grey let out a sigh of relief. It might take some extra practice, but he had a feeling they would make a great team.

Especially since they now had a secret weapon.

CHAPTER 8

After filling every remaining minute with practice, Grey and Ben headed to their cabin. Kiri would be sleeping in a different one with some of the other girl players. Hazel, who was already ranked in the thirties after her first day, teased Kiri as she went inside. It took everything for Grey not to say Hazel would regret that.

Players would figure out how good Kiri was eventually, but for now they had to keep Kiri's budding abilities secret. It would provide that much more advantage for them in tomorrow's battles.

Grey and Ben were the last to enter their cabin, and the other three guys stared at them as they chose their bunks. It turned out the "Lorenzo" on the cabin list was the football player who had also started that day. Tristan tried to pretend he'd forgotten who Ben and Grey were by only looking in the other direction.

And then there was the final guy, who must have been Tae Min.

Grey tried not to stare, but after what he'd already heard about Tae Min, it was hard not to want a peek at the guy no one could beat. The guy who could have gotten out the first season but was still here.

Tae Min was tall and thin, almost graceful as he arranged his area of the cabin. He had black hair that brushed his shoulders and hid part of his face. He seemed far more gentle than Grey expected, although Ben had described him as quiet. It was hard to picture this guy eliminating anyone in game. But everyone had counted Kiri out, too, and after the many times he got sniped tonight, Grey had a feeling she'd eventually be one of the best.

"Saw you took in that little baby girl," Lorenzo said with a laugh as he plopped into his bed. "You trying to lose harder?"

"Ben likes taking in strays," Tristan said. "Always has."

"Everyone deserves a chance," Ben growled back. "Aren't you glad your new squad gave you one, Tris? You've gone around begging for five seasons now."

"Ohhh, little guy's got some bite!" Lorenzo said with a laugh.

"So much for 'understanding,'" Tristan said to Ben.

"Just because I understand doesn't mean I have to like it." Ben leaned on the edge of the bed he'd chosen, glaring back at Tristan. "Will you come running back to me this time when they kick you out? That'll make you a stray, right?"

"I like this cabin!" Lorenzo watched with a strange sort of delight, his eyes moved to Grey. "You gonna get in on this prime smack talk, noob?"

"I'd rather let my abilities do the talking," Grey said.

"What abilities?" Tristan scoffed. "You get a couple kills and think you're great now."

"No," Grey hated this feeling in the room. The competition. The bragging. The fighting.

"But it's my first day. I'm going to practice, get better, and then my ranking and everyone else can do the talking for me."

"You'll never beat my ranking," Tristan said. "Ben's been trying that 'honest take' for five seasons and look where he is. Same place as always."

"We'll beat your squad," Ben said. "And then you'll see."

Tristan shook his head. "Go ahead and think that. You know it won't happen."

"We'll do it tomorrow," Ben said, his face now red from all the anger he held back. Grey worried he'd reveal just how talented Kiri was, but he didn't.

"Sure," Tristan held back a laugh. "I look forward to seeing that."

All players must be in bed in one minute!

Grey climbed into his bed since there wasn't much else to do. He didn't have to clean up—all that running didn't leave a single drop of sweat on him. Although after what Ben just said, he felt like he could sweat until his sheets were drenched. Maybe they could beat Tristan's new squad eventually, but tomorrow?

Grey would never fall asleep worrying about that. Their squad had potential, but he wasn't sure they had the kind of luck it would take to beat Tristan the very next day. But then, suddenly, his brain grew quiet and everything went blank.

As fast as Grey fell "asleep," he also awoke in a snap the next day. There were no dreams. No feeling of time having passed. It was the strangest thing to sit up in his bed and feel rested in the blink of an eye. He could see why the Admin made them take a break, even though they didn't have bodies in the traditional sense. After all the chaos of yesterday, his mind needed time to calm down. And he felt calmer.

At least until he remembered Ben's assertion that they'd beat Tristan today.

Battles commence in one hour!

"C'mon, Grey, let's find Kiri," Ben said.

"You gonna strategize on how to beat my squad?" Tristan asked.

Ben glared at him. "You aren't the only player in *Battle Royale*. We have to strategize on how to beat *everyone*."

"Let's just go." Grey grabbed Ben by the arm and pulled him out of the cabin and into the bright, unchanging sun. They didn't need to waste their time fighting with Tristan, and he had a feeling it would only get worse between them. "Don't let him get to you. You're right, we have to beat a lot of people."

"Why can't he just be cool about it?" Ben grumbled. "He doesn't have to rub it in my face. I thought we were . . ."

Friends. Grey had known Ben for only a day, but he knew that was what he'd say. Ben might have understood how the game worked and that it was ruthless, and yet it didn't stop him from caring about people. Grey thought that was an admirable quality, especially since it seemed like being stuck here had made a lot of people less caring and more like inescapable Internet trolls.

Speaking of trolls, Grey spotted Hazel and her squad standing around Kiri laughing at her.

"Have fun being last again today!" said a woman about Hazel's age. She had long black hair like Kiri, but it was straight instead. Hazel and the woman laughed with two other guys Grey didn't know.

"Thanks, Sandhya," Kiri grumbled.

"It's my personal goal to kill you first at least once today," Hazel said with a wicked grin. "Just give up now."

Kiri didn't look so strong or confident in the

face of this group. They were ranked in the thirties like Tristan's new group, and it seemed wrong to watch them pick on someone who wasn't even competition.

"Cut it out," Grey said, though everyone in the squad was much older than him. "Why don't you go smack talk someone your own rank? C'mon, Kiri."

Kiri ran over to them, her lip quivering like she was holding back tears. "There you are."

Hazel pushed back her short green hair. "You can tell me who to pick on when you manage to eliminate me, pipsqueak."

Grey wanted to be bold like Ben and say he could take out Hazel, but they didn't need to be the prime target of *two* top-forty squads.

"Ignore her, Grey," Ben jumped in. "Let's go practice a little more."

"So much practice," a guy in Hazel's squad said. "So little progress. How long have you been here again, Ben?"

"One season longer than you, Jamar!" Ben called back, though he didn't turn around. Grey didn't know which of the two guys on the squad was Jamar, but he figured he'd learn sooner or later.

"Why is everyone always so *mean*?" Kiri asked.

Ben sighed. "I don't know. Some seasons have been nicer than others. In season three, people really got on the 'teamwork' bandwagon. This one is shaping up to be cutthroat. Worse than season two."

"Wonderful," Kiri said as she stomped toward the practice warehouse. "At least I feel like I want to shoot everything today."

"Good." Grey followed her. He was ready to get some shooting done himself.

Before the battles began, everyone was teleported to the main warehouse the way they had started on the first day. They stood in the ranked line, and the Admin appeared in front of them like before.

"Welcome to Day Two of battles!" the Admin said. "To report on the state of the game—all items remain the same and there are no changes to the map. No glitches have been reported, and there are no impending patches to the current game. Should there be a patch, you will be informed of changes one week prior to the patch."

Grey raised an eyebrow. He hadn't realized that there might be changes to the game while he was living in it. That could be interesting. Maybe those "updates" happened when the players "slept."

"I wish you luck in today's battles," the Admin said. When she disappeared, the countdown for the first battle commenced.

Soon, Grey was back in the familiar air transportation and people began to jump out. The Battle Bus was packed even halfway through the drop, and Grey knew the reason immediately. The squads hazing them outside the game could tell who they were based on their skins, and they intended to make sure they trolled them inside the game, too.

"That's Tristan," Ben said to Kiri. "The one with the boring gear but the flashy pack. He's definitely revealing who we are to his squad so they can get guaranteed eliminations."

"So unfair," Kiri said.

"These other ones are probably Hazel's squad," Grey said. They wore special skins that not only changed their clothes, but also locked in different hairstyles and faces as well. He had a feeling the green-haired girl with pigtails was Hazel, since she wouldn't be afraid to flaunt her identity in game.

At least Hazel's squad couldn't talk to Grey's and they didn't have to hear all their mean comments. They just had to worry about Hazel's squad eliminating them.

"What are we supposed to do?" Kiri asked. "Hazel really will kill me first. She spent every minute insulting me last night until we got forced to sleep."

"We get Tristan's and Hazel's squads to shoot at each other first," Ben said with confidence. "They think it'll be fun to wreck us, but they'll worry about their own rank more. They're more of a threat to each other than we are to them."

"That's true." Grey felt a little better with that in mind. "So if we just dodge and get out of their way, maybe we can pick off a few of them."

"Let's hit Fatal Fields. We can land on the tallest building and hopefully we'll find a sniper weapon for Kiri," Ben said.

"I'm in," Kiri said.

"Going!" Ben jumped. Grey and Kiri followed right behind him. And sure enough, several people followed them out. Ben rushed for the farm and its cluster of buildings. He pulled out his glider to further guide his flight, and Grey tried to follow to the best of his best ability.

He also tried not to look back at all the people out to get them, but he was scared they would tail them right to the barn roof. He reminded himself they would need gear as well if they wanted to eliminate them. Some of the squad's members would spread out to find items before they circled back.

The moment they landed on the barn, Grey used his pickaxe to break down the roof. Kiri was a bit slow but had hers out soon enough. No one had landed there with them. Grey imagined they would be on the ground floor picking up weapons to kill them with.

There was a big gold chest right in front of them, and they opened it to find just what they were hoping to find—a sniper rifle for Kiri.

"Sweet as!" She grabbed it and the accompanying ammo. "Can I have the shield, too?"

"Yeah. Grey, take the grenades," Ben said. "I'll deal with the pistol."

"Okay." Grey grabbed the five grenades, hoping they'd come in handy. He heard destruction downstairs, so someone else was definitely there, although he wasn't sure which squad.

"There might be more items over here." Ben ran for the opposite side of the upper barn, where there was an alcove behind some bales of hay. Sure enough, there was a chest there as well. They opened it to find a blue AR, bandages, and some more ammo.

It wasn't a bad start. Too bad there were at least eight people after them.

"Back on the roof?" Grey asked after they looted up.

"Yeah." Ben used the wood he'd gotten from breaking the roof to build a ramp back up, and just in time, too, because someone busted the flooring and shots poured through the opening. Grey wanted to cover his ears, they were so loud at this short distance.

Kiri screamed as she ran, since the panic of nearby opponents was still an issue for her. They needed to get some distance. Grey threw one grenade out. It exploded without hitting anyone, but their enemies stayed back. He threw another, and this time he got someone down.

"One down!" he called out.

"Eliminate her before they revive!" Ben said

Grey unloaded his grenades on the squad, and they scattered away from their downed teammate. The person's items spilled from their body, and a shocking sentence appeared in Grey's vision:

You eliminated Hazel.

She was the first to be eliminated in the battle. Grey had a feeling he'd pay for that, but it still felt good after all Hazel's bragging and mean words. He ran up the ramp to the roof, where Ben was breaking down pieces to use for building. "Who's the first eliminated now?"

Kiri laughed. "Yeah, but we gotta get outta here."

"I need a weapon," Grey said. Hazel had dropped a decent machine gun, but her squad took it and he didn't dare face them all. "I'm out of grenades."

"Take the pistol until—" Ben started, but then a loud sound came from behind them. "No!"

"What?" Kiri said.

"Rocket launcher! Run!" Ben jumped off the roof, but before Grey and Kiri could, the shot landed right on them. The roof exploded into materials. Grey fell to the ground on his hands and knees in "downed state," but Kiri's shield kept her barely alive. She jumped for shelter, her health flashing dangerously low.

Since Grey was in a squad, he could crawl around and hope to get in a spot where his squad could revive him. So he tried to get off the roof where his team jumped, but then he heard the second rocket. He was a sitting duck.

And then he was a dead duck.

Tristan eliminated you.

"That lucky punk got a rocket launcher right off?" Ben yelled. "Figures."

"Well, that's the game, isn't it?" Grey said, though he wished for once he'd be the one to get the good item at the start.

"Rigged," Kiri grumbled. "Sorry, Grey."

"Just try to live as long as you can," Grey said. "I was the tenth down, so your rank will already improve, Kiri."

"Right. But yours won't," she replied.

"There are plenty more games." Grey tried to believe it. If they had five games a day for two months, that was around three hundred games. He couldn't panic after only six games. No one could get comfortable after so few.

As evidenced by Hazel's early demise in this game.

Ben and Kiri didn't last much longer. Tristan's

group had their number, and they took them down before they could escape Fatal Fields.

The moment the battle was over, Grey prepared for what might happen when they all came back to the warehouse. Everyone would be there, which meant Hazel and her squad would be waiting after he had eliminated her first. He wished that would shut her up, but he had a feeling it would do the opposite.

"Grey!" Hazel's voice sounded like his mom's when she was really mad.

He didn't have time to find Kiri or Ben. Grey broke into a sprint, leaving the warehouse through the nearest exit. He could still hear Hazel's voice yelling for him. But he was faster than Hazel outside the battle, where their avatar's speeds were regulated to make it fair.

"Come back here so I can teach you a lesson!" she screamed.

Grey went for the practice warehouse and grabbed a few weapons. Then he planned to run for the hills as fast as he could.

"Where are you going?" Ben cried as he and Kiri caught up to him. He hadn't even noticed they were following him.

"Hiding from Hazel!" If he could hide from her, that was his plan for at least the rest of the day. "I don't need to hear what she has to say about those grenades!"

Ben and Kiri both laughed. And Kiri said, "Good thinking, mate!"

"I know a good spot," Ben said. "She won't know it because she's new."

Ben guided Grey and Kiri to a river between two steep hills. There was a cave there, and Grey would have been afraid to go in if he didn't know this was a video game and there wouldn't be a bear.

"It wasn't the best first game, but I think we can do this," Ben said as he sat down on a rocky ridge. "And it sure was great to kill Hazel first."

Grey smiled. "So worth it."

"Guess you can tell her who to stop picking on now," Kiri said with laugh.

"I doubt she'll listen," Grey admitted. Though the battle wasn't a great rank at all, there was still something about it that made it different from yesterday. He wasn't as stressed out. He might even say he had fun. "I liked how we worked as a team, though. It was nice of you to give people weapons that fit them, Ben. I think that works a lot better than Tristan just getting all the good stuff."

Ben nodded. "I think so, too."

"We just have to get luckier with drops," Grey said.

"And we need more time to set up." Kiri leaned on the wall near Ben, her face serious but not upset. "How do we get them off our tails? They know us by our rubbish gear. They'll definitely target us next battle, too."

"Let's all go back to default settings," Ben said. "Sometimes the top players wear it, too, so they don't stand out."

"My friend Finn does that!" Grey chimed in. "He pretends to be a noob and makes himself look like a default character."

Ben smiled. "Wish he was here to help us out."

Grey felt a pinch of homesickness. "Me, too."

"If we jump in the first batch of players," Ben continued, "it'll be harder to figure out who is who. Even if they try to follow us, they have a much higher chance at guessing wrong."

"I like that," Grey said. "Where should we go next?"

"I know we've already tried the location, but

there's a cliff with a house on it just outside of Fatal Fields," Ben said. "It's got some decent gear, and it's a good lookout spot."

"May as well," Kiri said. "They might not think we'd try the same area twice."

"It's a plan then," Grey said. He tried not to smile, but he liked playing with Ben and Kiri. If in real life he'd gotten to play with them outside of this hacked *Battle Royale*, he'd want to keep playing with them. It was fun.

And that was something.

CHAPTER 9

It was only the second battle of the day, but Grey had a good feeling about it. Maybe it was the kill on Hazel giving him a confidence boost, or maybe it was just the way his team was working together. While Tristan was a good player, he wasn't a *team* player. Now they all were, and it took the edge off of being stuck in a game.

Not that Grey wanted to be trapped in *Battle Royale* forever, but having a few friends would make the ordeal much more bearable.

The moment the Battle Bus opened, Grey, Ben, and Kiri jumped from the bus with the majority of people. With a handful of others wearing default skins, it was much harder to tell who was who if you weren't in their squad.

Fatal Fields was on the opposite side of the map from where they soared through the sky, but they covered a lot of ground in flying. Many people dropped to different sites on the map as they continued on their course. Tilted Towers was where half the players went, and the others dropped down in groups after that.

This time, no one followed them like before, so their plan to jump early worked out. Maybe they would have a chance to establish themselves before the fighting began.

Ben pulled out his glider, and Grey did the same. They pushed forward toward Fatal Fields, but this time Grey saw the house on the hill that Ben had mentioned. As usual, Ben aimed for the roof, but then he let out a big gasp.

"What?" Kiri's voice sounded panicked. "Is someone there already?"

"No! Look!" Ben insisted.

Grey narrowed his eyes, trying to see what Ben could be so worked up about. The house wasn't broken, nor was anything on the hill. But then he spotted a purple thing on the open lawn in front of the house. Now Grey was the one gasping. "It's a llama!"

"A llama?" Kiri laughed. "This is about a silly llama?"

"It's a piñata filled with supplies!" Grey said. "No weapons, but lots of really good stuff and a ton of it! This is our lucky battle!"

"Ohhhh! Okay!" Kiri said. "Let's bust that open, ay?"

"You bet!" Ben landed in front of the llama and began hitting it with his pickaxe.

Grey joined in, and soon enough the llama broke and gave up its treasures. He couldn't help but smile as he took in all the ammo, materials, shields, and bandages. There was also a launch pad, which could be used to jump into the air and deploy your glider again, and several traps.

"Kiri, take the heavy bullets," Ben said. "They go with the sniper weapons. There's plenty of ammo. What do you want, Grey?"

"Let's split the medium and hope there are ARs in the house." Grey picked up the ammo. "You can have that rocket launcher ammo—maybe if we get one, you can show Tristan how to use it."

"Thanks," Ben said with a smile. "I'll take the materials, too, since I guess I can build the fastest."

"Sounds good, I'll grab the launch pad and traps," Grey said. After dividing the ammo and other items, they did the same with the bandages and shields. Grey already felt better equipped than he ever had—except for the fact that they needed weapons—and they hadn't even looted the house yet. They hurried inside and found three more chests. None were as great as the llama, but they yielded just what they needed.

"A bolt-action sniper!" Ben said with excitement. "That's the one for you, Kiri."

Kiri picked it up. "Pretty flash as, ay?"

"One down," Grey said, "Two or more weapons to go."

They ransacked the rest of the house, finding the two ARs they needed, although one wasn't as great as the other one. And then, in the final box, they found something that made Ben laugh.

"Seriously? A rocket launcher? We are so lucky." He picked it up. Grey and Kiri didn't argue with him. It felt right that he should have it after the last battle. "No wasting this opportunity, guys."

"No way," Grey said. They hadn't seen a single person yet, but there were already twenty eliminated players.

Storm approaches in two minutes and thirty seconds!

Grey checked the map, and the eye of the storm was perfectly situated over them. He couldn't help but smile. "We could set up here for a while if we wanted."

"Let's build a big tower for Kiri to snipe from," Ben said.

"We'll need more mats, even if we got some from the llama," Kiri said. "I don't have anything."

"Better farm up fast and come back," Ben said.

Grey couldn't help but feel nervous as they moved down from their high ground toward Fatal Fields. But there were plenty of trees to gather wood from, and they could possibly gather a few more backup weapons if Fatal Fields hadn't been looted fully.

They beat down trees on their way, and Grey soon had over three hundred wood. As they approached the fields, Grey switched to his AR and kept his eye out for other players.

Sure enough, he spotted someone beyond the barn. Without thinking, he let off shots. Numbers for damage shone, and soon the player was downed.

"Finish them," Ben said. "I'm looking out for the other ones."

"Got it." The extra damage from a good gun made it easy for Grey to take out the player.

You eliminated Martine.

It wasn't a name he knew, but he'd take any win over any player.

"Roof!" Kiri said. She had her sniper out, and in one shot the enemy fell to the ground. "Oh! Head shot! Ha."

"Nice!" Ben said as he used his weapon to finish off the roof player.

Ben eliminated Coco.

"Stealing my credit!" Kiri said.

"Sorry." Ben was already moving toward the building where the eliminated player left their items. He built a ramp so they could get up. "See anyone else?"

"No," Grey said. Either they were only paired as two, or the rest of their squad had left them for dead. The other loot was in the middle of the field, but he wasn't sure it was a good idea to go out in the open to get it. Coco had dropped a few rifles and another sniper, so that helped. "We don't have much time until the storm moves in. Then more people will be here."

"Yeah, let's move," Kiri said. "Do we have enough mats?"

"Could always use more," Ben said. "Never hurts to be maxed out."

The three hundred wood Grey had sure felt like enough, but he trusted Ben's experience. They broke down a few more trees on their way back up to the house on the hill.

As they climbed to their original location, the eye of the storm began to shrink. There was still a lot of space around them, since it was only the first storm movement, but Grey knew this would bring more players to the area. The number of eliminated players quickly rose from twenties to fifties as people tried to get to the safe zone.

But there was still some luck on their side, because the circle for the next storm was right on top of their area. They couldn't be in a better position.

Now all they needed was a tower.

Grey didn't have enough experience with the building tools, but he knew to start building four walls to protect them from all sides. Ben added a ramp, and they moved up a level. Kiri kept a lookout from the top, and when she started firing shots Grey began to panic that their tower would get destroyed right from under them.

Kiri eliminated Jamar.

"Great shot!" Ben said.

"Wait . . ." Grey's sense of dread only grew. "Wasn't Jamar on Hazel's squad?"

"Yeah, they're here," Ben said.

Kiri whimpered, "She's coming for me again."

"We're not building fast enough, are we?" Grey asked.

"I told you I'm not great at this part," Ben said nervously. "We just need a few more levels. And Kiri, watch above, too. Sometimes people build sky towers."

"Sky towers?" she squeaked.

Grey had seen it in videos. "Yeah, they load up on mats and build their stuff out in the sky."

"These people are mad," Kiri said as she took another few shots. "Who even thinks to do that?"

"Scrappy people," Ben said. "Just focus on your shooting, though. You're doing great."

Kiri eliminated Guang through head shot.

"See? You're on fire!" Grey said as he frantically tried to build their tower. He knew at least that no one had made it up their hill, but that didn't make him feel safe. There were other ways to get up higher. If it wasn't a sky tower, then it was the launch pad.

"There's two more, they must be Hazel and Sandhya," Kiri said. "But they've taken cover now. I think they're building up to us."

"Probably. This should be tall enough now. Let's build out a little." Ben began to lay down some floors in brick, which was stronger than wood but took longer to be fully built. "Be careful, they'll try to take out our floors and we'll fall and be eliminated."

"They're building so fast!" Kiri said. "They're almost at my eye level!"

"My turn then!" Ben ran to where Kiri peered out from behind their walls. He equipped his rocket launcher and let the rockets fly into their structure. The wood splintered to pieces on impact, and then after another two rockets Grey saw an ever-satisfying:

Ben eliminated Hazel.

Ben eliminated Sandhya.

"Yes!" Ben let out a long laugh. "She's gonna be so mad at us."

"And I'm stuck in her cabin! Thanks!" Kiri said.

With those four eliminated, it was clear they had taken out all of Hazel's squad. That was a big deal for a low-rank group like Grey's. Only twenty people remained on the map, and Grey couldn't believe that included them.

It also included Tristan's new squad.

Grey didn't have much hope for a Victory Royale, but he really, really wanted to beat Tristan's squad at the very least. He wanted to prove to everyone on the map that he and Kiri and Ben shouldn't be written off. They weren't going to give up and accept low ranks.

The eye of the storm began to shrink again, and Grey checked the map to see if they would have to move. To his shock, the next zone was *still* right on top of them. It couldn't have been more perfect.

"Kiri, cover us while we go get that gear Hazel and Sandhya dropped," Ben said.

"Right."

Instead of going down their tower, Ben just built over to the one that Hazel's squad had made. Grey gathered the ammo for his weapons and picked up the shields and bandages. Ben upgraded his AR with a better one, and they found several traps and a grenade launcher that would come in handy to defend their tower.

"Incoming!" Kiri called. "From above and below!"

Grey looked up, and sure enough, there was a path in the sky made from wood. Four people ran on it, but they looked like ants from this distance. They wouldn't be in range for any shots, so they'd have to wait until they came down closer.

They'd have to get the players below first.

Kiri was already shooting at them, since the storm was closing in on that side and their enemies were taking damage. Grey joined in, and together they eliminated three players. The fourth took too much damage from the storm and was eliminated, too.

Tristan still hadn't been eliminated, and there were only eight players left.

That meant it was Tristan's squad versus theirs, plus Tae Min, most likely. While Grey couldn't guess where Tae Min would be, it was obvious that Tristan was up above in the sky.

As the storm indicated it would shrink right over Grey's squad, he saw Tristan's squad begin to build down.

"We're in trouble," Grey said. "They have the high ground."

"We just have to be patient," Ben said. "Wait until my call, and we all unload at once. If they fall they're doomed."

Kiri took a deep breath, looking through her scope. "Four hundred meters . . . three-ninety . . ."

Ben pulled out his rocket launcher, and Grey opted for the grenade launcher he'd grabbed off Hazel. The eye of the storm was such a small radius at this point it would be hard to dodge. Tristan's squad began to open fire on them, and Grey took a hit that killed most of his shield.

"Now!" Ben yelled.

Grey launched all the grenades he had, while Ben shot off the remainder of his rockets. Kiri kept shooting, but instead of aiming for the players she went for their floor. The structure crumbled under them, and Grey could hardly believe it as he watched the whole squad fall to the ground.

He couldn't see where they fell past the hill they staked out, but he knew they weren't eliminated yet because it wasn't announced. At least one of them had survived the fall somehow and was probably trying to revive their squad.

"Hurry! We gotta get them before they revive each other!" Ben built a ramp down to the top of the hill, and they rushed to get a good angle on them. Sure enough, one of them had been able to build a ramp that must have saved them from taking full damage. But before Grey's squad could get them, a spam of eliminations appeared on the screen.

Tae Min eliminated Farrah.

Tae Min eliminated Hans.

Tae Min eliminated Mayumi.

Tae Min eliminated Tristan.

"Dang! I wanted that kill so bad!" Ben said. "Oh well."

Tae Min stood at the edge of the storm on the ground, and Grey stared at him in awe. He probably should have thought of shooting, but part of him wondered if he'd ever witness this moment again. Like Ben had said, Tae Min didn't wear any fancy skins. He didn't stand out, even though he probably had the pick of every skin at rank 1.

What was stranger was that Tae Min didn't shoot back at them, either. He watched them like Grey watched him. Grey couldn't guess what Tae Min was thinking, but before he could act, a bullet came soaring out of nowhere and got Tae Min.

Kiri eliminated Tae Min by head shot.

Victory Royale!

Before Grey could even process what had

happened, he was back in the cave where they had hidden from Hazel. "Did we just *win?*"

"Yeah! Kiri just head shot Tae Min!" Ben shook his head in disbelief. "I can't believe you did that."

"He was just standing there!" Kiri said. "Isn't that what I'm supposed to do?"

Ben began laughing. "Yeah, but it was *Tae Min!*"

Kiri shrugged.

Ben only laughed harder. And Grey joined in, as the reality of winning sank in. Maybe half of it was luck, but they actually beat all the other squads. They beat Tae Min. And if it could happen once, that meant it could happen again.

Maybe he wouldn't be stuck here forever after all.

CHAPTER 10

The remaining three games didn't go half as well as their second game, but Grey wasn't complaining. All of them finished the day ranked in the fifties, and that felt like a victory when everyone thought they'd be at the bottom.

The Admin appeared to give her usual speech. "Congratulations on completing Day Two. Your ranks are posted on the wall. All established protocol must be followed unless otherwise indicated. Good night."

Grey smiled as he looked at his rank of 51. So did Kiri, who had jumped from the nineties to rank 59. It was amazing what a Victory Royale could do for ranks.

"Not bad, ay?" Kiri said. "Thanks for helping me."

"You helped us," Grey said. "You racked up the kills."

"We did better today than we did with Tristan," Ben chimed in. "That teamwork. So underrated."

Grey smiled. It felt good to improve in rank, but it felt even better to do it as a team. He was glad he didn't have to do it alone.

"You're going down tomorrow!" Hazel yelled from across the warehouse. "That was luck only!"

None of them said anything back. It was kind of true, but also Grey didn't want to aggravate someone like Hazel more than necessary. He was relieved when she stomped out of the warehouse instead of coming to confront them more. But then he spotted someone else heading their way, and that might have been worse.

Tristan.

Grey braced himself for more trolling, but then he realized Tristan didn't look so much mad as he did upset.

"What's up?" Ben said with a hint of a smile.

"You guys did good today," Tristan said as he

glanced at Kiri. "Everyone is talking about your sniper. She might get recruited."

"I'm not going anywhere," Kiri said.

"Well, don't speak too soon," Tristan said and he looked down at his feet. "My squad kicked me out so they could try to get you instead. Good snipers are rare, and you're not even trained."

"They kicked you out?" Ben raised his eyebrows. "After one day?"

"Our rank dropped ten points," Tristan said. "They're blaming it on me."

Grey didn't know whether to feel sorry or to feel like Tristan got what he deserved. But either way, it was a cruddy position to be in. Grey looked to Ben, wondering if he'd say what he thought he might say.

"Well, if you want to hang out with a buncha noobs, we still have a spot," Ben said. "But Grey and Kiri would have to be cool with it. And we work as a team, you're not the boss."

Kiri raised an eyebrow. "I guess if you can stomach him, Ben, I can."

Ben looked to Grey. "What do you think?"

Part of Grey wanted to say no, but Tristan was also a good player. Not the most loyal, but maybe he had learned his lesson. Grey hoped he wouldn't regret it, but he said, "Everyone deserves a second chance, right?"

Ben nodded. "Or a thirtieth."

"Hey," Tristan said. "It's more like twenty. Sorry, man. I just . . ."

"We all want to get home," Ben said. "I know."

"Yeah . . ." Tristan turned bright red.

"Maybe we can do that together?" Grey chimed in. "There are five spots and four of us. We don't have to sell each other out to all go home this season."

"That's the spirit!" Kiri said.

Grey looked around at his squad, feeling better than ever. It would still be hard to make it home this season, but what felt impossible two days ago didn't seem so bad in this moment. He could get home. It would take work. A lot of luck. And a heavy helping of teamwork. But he could do it.